For my family, my gift. — G.B.

For the ones who taught me the art of giving and the
beauty of receiving — my family. — A.M.

AUTHOR'S NOTE

In the story, people "give back" to others by participating in a community drive and dinner,
but there are lots of ways to show someone you care. Inviting a new friend to play at recess,
cheering on a teammate, making holiday cards for seniors in your neighborhood, or even
sharing a welcoming smile can brighten another person's day.

— Gina Bellisario

10 9 8 7 6 5 4 3 2 1   24 25 26 27 28 · Printed in China 38 · First edition, September 2024 · Book design by Rae Crawford
The text type was set in Iowan Old Style. The display type was set in Alice. · The illustrations were created digitally using Adobe Photoshop.

Give Back

Community
food drive
and dinner

Donations and
volunteers needed.
6 pm at the Community Center

by Gina Bellisario   *illustrated by* Alicia Más

ORCHARD BOOKS
An Imprint of Scholastic Inc. • New York

Community
food drive
and dinner

Donations and
volunteers needed.

6pm at the Community Center

GIVE
BACK
LOVE
DOWN

Greet the morning shiny-new,
seat for me and seat for you,
drip-drop syrup, pancake stack.

Take a plate, and . . .

give back.

Find a teddy fuzzy-brown,
princess castle, sparkling crown,
puppets, puzzles, train and track.

Love the toys, and . . .

give back.

Pick some mittens soft and snug,
cozy sweater, comfy hug,
extra jacket off the rack.

Add the clothes, and . . .

give back.

Borrow a wagon rosy-red,
blossoms from a blooming bed.
Sneak a crunchy cookie snack.

Share a moment, and . . .

give back.

Ding-dong doorbells fill the air.
Kindness rings out everywhere.
Giving neighbors, growing sack.

Collect the gifts, and . . .

give back.

Load the boxes piled high,
brightening streetlamps, dimming sky,
helping hands to pack and pack.

Catch a ride, and . . .

give back.

Grab an apron, silver scoop,
supper tray and piping soup.
Caring hearts and thoughtful acts.

Fill the bowls, and . . .

give back.

Give back warmth, a sweet embrace.

Give back joy, a smiling face.

Give back what you can and then . . .

see your good come back again.